The Parable of Young Albert

Written by Lynne Preston

BOSTOCK HOUSE PUBLISHING

ESTABLISHED 2025

Hardcover ISBN: 978-1-0693280-0-7

Paperback ISBN: 978-1-0693280-2-1

E-Book ISBN: 978-1-0693280-1-4

Bostock House Publishing

First Published 2025

Info@Bostock-House-Publishing.com

For all those who enjoy a good yarn

The Parable of Young Albert

Written by Lynne Preston

Table of Contents

Table of Contents

Cast of Characters

Young Albert	An Upright Citizen
Miss Suki	Young Albert's Companion
The Landlady	Proprietor; the 'Den of Inik Witty'
Daphne	The 'Meals on Wheels' Lady
Gertrude	The Head Postmistress
Persephone	The School Ma'am
Mousey-Looking Lady	Busy-Body at Large
The Courier	Local Delivery Driver
Mrs. Brown	Post Office Customer
Tom	Bolder Lad at the Local Pub
The Cellar Lad	The Landlady's Assistant
Constable Howard	The Local Bobby
The Young Mother	One of the Neighbours
Incidental Characters	In the Pub or Behind Curtains

The Parable of Young Albert
Introduction
Young Albert

This is a tale concerning Young Albert... well, I say 'Young Albert' although at the time of this tale he was no longer so young. It was his dad, you see, his name had been Old Albert so, naturally, his offspring was and indeed still is, known as 'Young Albert'.

Well, Young Albert lived in a small village in the depths of the Cotswolds. The village, Rowhampton-on-Severn, was much as it had been in the 1920's; fresh farm milk, eggs and bacon being delivered by horse and cart bright and early every morning, the baker and his lad hot on the milkman's heels in their van. The mail was delivered twice a day by a portly fellow on a little red motorbike and the local Bobby still walked the beat. Oh, yes, it was a quaint village was Rowhampton-on-Severn. Life went on at a gentile pace...and there was not much that went unnoticed; although Young Albert's malady seemed to have been missed.

Young Albert, you see, was coming up to his seventy-fifth birthday and had, for some months, been feeling, well... for want of a better phrase... 'Out of Sorts'.

Not that there was anything wrong with his health, on the contrary, Young Albert was as healthy as a horse and, in his own right, as fit as the proverbial butcher's dog. No, the cause of Young Albert's malady was to do with the fact that, for the past quarter-of-a-century, he had been living on his Jack Jones. It was his wife you see, Mrs. Posthelwaite (for that was Young Albert's name, Young Albert Posthelwaite) had buggered off with the Head Post Mistress's husband all those many years ago.

Not that Young Albert blamed the Head Post Mistress's husband, he'd have buggered off himself if that harpy had been his wife. No, he didn't blame him for buggaring off, but why did he have to take Mrs. Posthelwaite with him?

Well, what was done was done and there was no use in crying over milk that had already been spilt. Young Albert though, as has been mentioned earlier, had been feeling 'Out of Sorts' just lately.

So then, the crux of the matter is that his sister's granddaughter loved those dainty Japanese Dolls that you see here and there and so Young Albert had determined to get one for her eighth birthday. Nothing wrong with that, nothing wrong with that at all. However, Young Albert was a bit of a Luddite when it came to using computers and t'internet so it had been a bit of a hit and miss job for him to run down the right item and, on his journey, he had come across something interesting... something very interesting indeed.

It seemed, to his fascination, that there was more to 'Japanese Dolls' than had previously met his eye.

Even so, determined to stick to his plan, he had indeed ordered an appropriate Japanese Doll for his sister's granddaughter and made arrangements for it to be delivered to her address up North in Manchester... and then he had backtracked to where he had seen these other types of Japanese Doll... or 'Companion Dolls' as he had persuaded himself to call them.

Yes, Young Albert had been fascinated and, after several sleepless nights and much deliberating had decided on one model in particular... known as 'Suki'... and had ordered her in the hopes that she would arrive for his upcoming birthday. In Young Albert's defence (should he need any) I must remind the reader that he had been on his Jack Jones for a quarter-of-a-century and, before he had retired from the silk mill in Turn, had never missed a day's work since he left school and had always minded his 'P's and 'Q's. On top of that, the eligible women of the village, although nice enough in their own way, had never shown any interest in him. Indeed, the only woman that visited his house was the 'Meals on Wheels' lady who showed up at his house once a week driving her ancient Morris Eight Van.

Delicious and welcome though the meals were, the 'Meals on Wheels' lady herself was not one to be desired; indeed not. The 'Meals on Wheels' lady, you see, was one of the 'Three Banshees'; the Head Postmistress and the School Ma'am being the other two.

The Parable of Young Albert

Chapter One

'The Den of Inik-Witty'

"Another Brown Fillup is it, Young Albert?"

"What? Oh, yes!" says Young Albert, roused from his reverie.

He was down at the 'George and Dragon' you see or, as it was now called, 'The Den of Inik-Witty', this being the Landlady's doing in an attempt to teach the 'Three Banshees' a lesson.

"I'll give you 'Den of Iniquity'!" she had yelled at them as they had paraded around with their bloody signs.

The Landlady had stormed up the ladder herself on that Saturday the year before, grabbed hold of the old pub sign and sent it skittering; the 'Three Banshees' doing the 'Hop-Skip-and-a-Jump' in a vain attempt to save their ankles from injury. The Landlady, with a nod of satisfaction, had lumbered back down the ladder and told the cellar lad to handle the rest. The rest being to put the new sign, 'The Den of Inik-Witty' in its place.

"Bloody Banshees!" she had yelled as they hobbled off down the street. All the lads had cheered as, smacking her hands together, she had stomped back into the bar.

Since then, the 'Three Banshees' and the Landlady had had an unofficial truce. The Landlady would tend to her own business and 'The Three Banshees' would tend to someone else's.

"There you go, Young Albert," the Landlady says, setting down his pint of mild and bottle of brown ale. Then, "Penny for them?"

"Er, what?"

"Your thoughts… penny for your thoughts."

"Oh, it's nowt," Young Albert replied. "Nowt at all, only it's my birthday coming up and I'm expecting a bit of company."

"Well," says the Landlady, with a smile. "Good for you… but don't go dancing the night away now."

As it happens, dancing was the subject on Young Albert's mind as he had sat there staring into space.

Dancing with 'Suki'… he knew he could teach her and, what's more, she was bound to let him take the lead.

Yes, he had such plans for himself and 'Suki'.

He could spin yarns for her as he sat over a pipe by the fireside in the evenings; tell her the happenings he observed on his morning walks; bring back some of the local gossip from the 'George'. He would make sure that she knew to beware of the 'Three Banshees' as well.

"Bloody 'ell," he muttered to himself, hefting his fresh pint of mild. "I'd better not let them buggars get wind of her."

The Parable of Young Albert
Chapter Two
Suki

In due course, Young Albert's birthday and Suki arrived… both on the same day as it happens. He had just got back from his morning walk when a courier van (causing tongues to wag behind chintz curtains) pulled up in front of his house.

Young Albert, feeling nervous, opened his front door as the courier came up the front path carrying a large box under one arm and a clipboard under the other.

"Delivery for Mister Albert Posthelwaite," he said, in a loud, clear voice that carried on the wind to the far reaches of the village. He set the box down on its end and consulted the clipboard. "Express from Akihabara Doll Works, Tokyo, Japan." He held out the clipboard to Young Albert. "If you will just sign here, sir?"

Young Albert, looking sheepish and glancing up and down the street, took hold of the proffered clipboard and pen and signed on the dotted line.

"Very good, sir!" the courier said, a twinkle in his eye. Then, with a quick salute, "Enjoy your day, sir."

Before Young Albert could think of a reply, the courier was striding back to his van whistling merrily.

Meanwhile, Young Albert wasted no time in getting his parcel into the house and out of sight of prying eyes.

Once inside, with the front door firmly locked, he laid the box down on the living room floor, closed the curtains and then sat in his armchair studying the box. For no reason he could explain, he still felt nervous, however, after a few minutes, he pulled himself together, got back to his feet and set about opening it.

In short order Young Albert, tossing the instructions aside (as all real men do) soon had his new friend out of the box and sitting in one of the armchairs by the fire. She was already dressed in the outfit she had appeared in when he had first seen her on the computer screen.

He sat down in the armchair opposite and, for a while, he just stared at her. Then, pulling himself together again, he cleared his throat and said, "Welcome home, Suki! I'll just put the kettle on."

On his way to the kitchen, he opened the front curtains. He would be buggared if he was going to spend the rest of his life in the dark.

At this point, I should point out to the reader that Young Albert's new companion resembled a young Asian woman in her mid-thirties. She wore a rather demure black skirt with white blouse and stylish red cardigan. On her feet, she wore black, low-heeled shoes. A gold bracelet with trinkets adorned her left wrist.

Young Albert, a smile on his face, was soon back with two cups of tea and a couple of biscuits on a tray. He placed one cup, biscuit on the saucer, at Suki's elbow then showed her the birthday cards he had received that morning. They were from his sister, his niece and her daughter. Surprisingly enough, there was also a business-like one from the 'Meals on Wheels' lady.

Settling down into his own armchair he said, "Well, Suki, I dare say as this is a lot different than what you're used to. You'll be alright though, Rowhampton-on-Severn is a quiet enough place and...well... once I've got the nerve up, we can go down the 'George and Dragon' of an evening."

Yes, Young Albert was determined to pluck up the courage to take Suki out and about. He just had to come up with the means to do it. After all, walking was not one of Suki's main attributes.

The Parable of Young Albert
Chapter Three
Trouble Brewing

After a lunch of cheese on toast and another cup of tea, Young Albert, after donning his tweed jacket and cap, told Suki that he was just nipping down the pub and that he would be back in about an hour.

Meanwhile, he advised that she herself should rest up and generally get over the jet-lag she was no doubt experiencing.

Before he left, Young Albert went over to her, kissed her on the forehead and closed her eyes.

Off he went then, light of heart and step, down the front path and off to the pub.

Little did he know that, although it wasn't her day, the 'Meals on Wheels' lady was lurking around the corner at the wheel of her trusty old van and, once Young Albert was out of sight, she pounced. She had got wind of him telling the Landlady that he was expecting company on his birthday and, being an old biddy, she had to get to the bottom of the matter. Find out just who this mysterious company was, visiting someone on her beat an' all.

With a grind of gears and slipping of clutch, up to the front of his house she drove, pulled up with a squeal of brakes and fair ran up the front path. Going straight to the living room window, noting with satisfaction that the old dodderer had left the curtains open, she cupped her hands round the sides of her face and pressed her fat little nose right up against the glass pane.

"Well, I'll be a Maiden Aunt," she gasped, eyes popping. "A Chinese girl!" Wasting no time, she trotted back to her van and then, breathlessly, drove to the village post office.

"Gertrude," she gasped, almost tripping over herself as she hurtled through the doorway. "Gertrude… He's a Chinese girl."

"What?" said the Head Postmistress, handing a parcel over the counter. "There you are Mrs. Brown," she said. "Give my regards to Mr. Brown."

With that, both the 'Banshees' waited until they had the post office to themselves. Immediately Mrs. Brown had left, the 'Meals on Wheels' lady closed and latched the door.

"Young Albert," she gasped again. "He's a Chinese girl."

"What? How can he be a Chinese girl? Come to the back room and sit down for goodness sake, before you do yourself an injury." The Head Postmistress led her friend around the post office counter. "There, now, sit you down while I put the kettle on."

"He has," Daphne said (Daphne for that, as is now revealed, was the name of the 'Meals on Wheels' lady) "Young Albert… got himself a Chinese girl he has."

"Ah!" said Gertrude with an air of enlightenment. "He has a Chinese girl. He is not one himself."

"Of course he's not one himself," Daphne said, somewhat scornfully. "There she is, big as life, in Mrs. Postlethwaite's armchair. Dozing by the fireside, if you please."

Gertrude, at the mention of Mrs. Postlethwaite, bristled but then decided to let it go as, after all, it was a long time ago and this sounded like too juicy a story to miss.

"Dozing in Mrs. Postlethwaite's armchair you say?"

"Big as life, Gertrude! Big as life."

"Indeed?" The Head Postmistress handed her friend a cup of tea, then sipped from her own cup. "Well, Daphne, I don't think we can have that?"

"Course we can't have that!" the Meals on Wheels lady replied. "It's not right, letting her run roughshod all over Mrs. Postlethwaite's front room carpet like that."

"Not right at all," said the Head Postmistress. Then, decisively, "We'll have a meeting at Persephone's house tonight right soon as she comes out of school."

"Right!" Daphne agreed.

"We'll soon put a stop to this nonsense. Old dodderer like him carrying on like that."

The Parable of Young Albert
Chapter Four
A Quiet Jug of Ale

Young Albert, of course, was quite oblivious to all this as he sat at his corner table showing a Brown Fillup the way home.

"Company arrived alright?" the Landlady said, busily polishing a pint pot. There were not many customers at this time of day, although there was one of particular note... a mousey-looking woman in a tan raincoat sitting at the long bench, back to the window. Her ears had pricked up on hearing the Landlady's query.

Young Albert paused, jug of ale halfway to his mouth.

"Oh, aye! Company's arrived alright. She's having a nap... getting over her journey you know."

"Yes, best way." The Landlady considered then said, "I see as the courier was at your house this morning as well."

At this, the mousey-looking lady put her glass of Vimto to her lips in the pretense of sipping from it. She was, however, all ears.

"Oh, aye!" Young Albert repeated. "Brought me a birthday present." He took a good pull on his pint, then put the jug back down on the table, topping it up from the bottle of brown ale.

"From Tokyo as I heard," the Landlady said, pressing him.

"Er... Who's that?" said Young Albert, evasively. "The courier?"

"No, you soft 'ap'orth, the present."

"Aye well, I dare say as near everything's made in Japan in this day and age."

At this (and as the mousey-looking lady, having abandoned her Vimto, scuttled to the door) the Landlady decided to let the matter drop, but she knew something was afoot and, although she was not cut from the same cloth as the 'Three Banshees' she still had her share of curiosity.

≈ ≈ ≈ ≈ ≈

"I'm home!" Young Albert called out as he entered the house. He took off his tweed jacket and cap, hung them up on the peg by the door and went into the living room. Suki, he was pleased to see, was still napping by the fireside.

He went to the bathroom, looked in the mirror and rubbed his chin. He decided that a shave was in order as he wanted to look his best for when Suki woke up.

He hummed a tune and did a little dance as he ran the electric razor over his cheeks. When he had finished, he rooted out a bottle of aftershave that he had last used he couldn't remember when. After a bit of a struggle getting the top off, he dabbed a few drops around the backs of his ears then rubbed his hands dry on the sides of his trousers.

"Well, you're an old fool," he said, looking himself over in the bathroom mirror. "Ah, well!" he shrugged. "No fool like an old fool."

With that, he went back to the kitchen, pulled out a frozen Meals-on-Wheels dinner from the freezer, took it out of the carton and put it to cook in the microwave oven. Mashed potatoes, roast beef and peas. He also had a little birthday cake in the fridge, he had bought it the day before from the baker's van.

"Ah!" he said, walking into the living room, leaning over Suki and opening her eyes. "Just in time for tea."

Gently, he lifted Suki, took her over to the table and sat her in a chair. He put her hands on the edge of the table. "I hope you don't mind English food," he said, by way of conversation. "I don't go in for any fancy cooking myself."

Although he had prepared a small plate for Suki he did have to, after he had eaten, give her a helping hand.

The main part of the meal over, he collected up the plates and dumped them into the sink.

He brought the birthday cake out of the fridge, stuck a candle in the top of it, lit it and carried it over to the table singing, "Happy Birthday to Me!"

"You're all I'm wishing for today," he said, looking Suki in the eyes and treating her to a warm smile. "I'm glad you got here in time for my birthday."

The Parable of Young Albert
Chapter Five
The Day After the Day Before

Young Albert, having had the most restful night's sleep in a quarter-of-a-century, woke up with a contented smile on his face. He raised himself up on one elbow; wondered if Suki had slept just as well in her room (for separate rooms so it was) then became aware of the most awful racket.

From the street that ran by his house there came a terrible caterwauling and carrying on. An ear-shattering din assaulting his ears. For an instant Young Albert thought that it was maybe a couple of Tom cats going at it, or rather that's what he hoped. But no... when he threw the curtains open a terrible sight greeted his eyes. It was as he had feared.

Down on the ancient cobbles, the 'Three Bloody Banshees' were parading up and down outside his house, banners and signs held aloft bearing the slogans of self-righteous anger.

'Shameful'

'A Crime Against Humanity'

'A Downright Disgrace'

'Barbaric'

'An Outrage'

'Degenerate Debauchee'

'Have You No Scruples?'

'We're Thinking of Mrs. Postlethwaite!'

Meanwhile, the 'Three Banshees' themselves were chanting, "The Doll must Go! The Doll must Go!"

Yes, from putting the pieces of gossip together… the courier and the parcel, their tan-raincoated quisling reporting the words of the Landlady and Young Albert's remark of, "'Aye well, I dare say as near everything's made in Japan in this day and age.'" they had managed to work out that the Chinese Girl was in fact a Japanese Doll… and it was nothing short of a bloody disgrace. That and the fact that Mrs. Postlethwaite was only just recently out of the house… and who could blame her?

"A Bloody Disgrace!" the three of them howled in unison as Young Albert, still in his pyjamas, peered from the bedroom window.

"It's Disgusting!"

Well there was nothing Young Albert could do, apart from shuffle the curtains back together and get dressed for the day.

On his way to the stairs, he looked in on Suki in the room he had prepared for her at the back of the house. She was still fast asleep and dreaming of who knew what.

"Them three pursed-lipped shrews," he muttered. "Can't stand for anybody to be happy."

Well, at least they had not managed to disturb Suki's sleep. He closed her bedroom door then went down to the kitchen to get breakfast on the go.

He was at a loss regarding what to do about the 'Three Banshees'. They were parading around on a public street, so he doubted he could move them on. He knew the local Bobby wouldn't dare do anything about it either; not while the School Ma'am was his Great Aunt.

The Parable of Young Albert
Chapter Six
The Landlady

Thankfully it was a weekday so, by nine in the morning, the 'Three Banshees', after one last howl of, "It's a Damn Disgrace!" had left the scene.

Through the living room window, Young Albert, interrupting his conversation with Suki, noticed the young mother across the road come scurrying out of the house to bundle her children into the car. He shook his head and tut-tutted. Looks like they would be late for school. No doubt the School Ma-am would have something to say about that, even though it was partly her doing.

He was about to turn his attention back to Suki when the Landlady hove into view. She was pushing along an old wheelchair.

One moment, Suki," he said, getting to his feet. "It looks like we have a visitor."

He was already opening the front door as the doorbell chimed.

"Well, if it isn't the Landlady," he said, smiling and glancing down at the wheelchair. "This is a surprise."

"Aye well," the Landlady replied. "There's talk all over the village and I thought as my Dennis's old wheelchair might come in handy for you." She looked away and wiped a tear from her eye. "It's of no use to him now, after all."

"Well, I… I don't know what to say. Better come in," Young Albert said, standing aside from the door.

The Landlady, rattling her Dennis's old wheelchair through the doorway, followed Young Albert to his kitchen/dining room.

"So this is your company," she said, smiling at Suki.   "Er, yes… Suki, this is the Landlady."

"Well, I'm pleased to meet you, Miss Suki," the Landlady said, then turned her attention back to Young Albert.

"Cup of tea?" he said, lifting the teapot. "Fresh brewed not ten minutes ago."

"Maybe another time, Young Albert. I have to get back to the pub, the cellar lad you know. Not all that bright."

"Aye, well, I won't comment on that."

Young Albert showed his guest to the front door and, as she was leaving, she said, over her shoulder, "Why not bring Miss Suki to the Inn for Sunday lunch?" She nodded towards the wheelchair standing in the passageway. "After all, you have the means now."

"I'll think on that, Landlady… and thank you."

The Parable of Young Albert
Chapter Seven
Sunday Lunch

Thursday came and went and Friday followed suit, the 'Three Banshees' holding protests outside Young Albert's house from seven in the morning 'til just before nine. They had even come up with a couple of more signs:

'Young Albert the Barbarian'

and

'Run Him Out on a Rail'

During this time, there had been no sign of Constable Howard. Young Albert had, on the Friday morning, made a phone call to the main constabulary in Turn, the closest sizeable town to Rowhampton-on-Severn, only to be informed that Constable Howard had been called in for further training and, unless it was an emergency, could it wait until Monday morning?

Well, at least Saturday morning had been peaceful as on that day, the 'Three Banshees' were wont to crowd into the 'Meals on Wheels' lady's Morris Eight van and go up to the Market at Turn. No doubt tuning Constable Howard in on the latest outrage as well.

As for Sunday, well, those guardians of morality always went to church and from there to the house of whoever's turn it was to make lunch. This then gave Young Albert the chance to make good on the Landlady's invitation. He had told Suki about the 'George and Dragon' and change of name.

He fancied that Suki had laughed at this, but she was so demure he couldn't be certain. However, around eleven o' clock on Sunday morning they were both ready to go. Suki still had but the one outfit so, in order to keep her warm, Young Albert draped one of his old sports jackets over her shoulders and, once he had her sitting comfortably, he placed an English wool blanket over her legs then manoeuvred her and the wheelchair out the front door.

"I think you'll enjoy this, Suki," he said, as he pushed her down the front path. "In fact, I think we both will."

It didn't take long, and with only the odd set of chintz curtains rustling, before Young Albert and his Oriental friend were entering the 'Den of Inik Witty'. The Landlady herself hurried over to greet them.

"Come in! Come in!" she said. "I've kept your usual table for you, Young Albert." This, although being a nice gesture, was totally unnecessary as no-one else fancied Young Albert's usual table, being tucked away in the corner as it was.

Wanting to give the full treatment the Landlady led the way and, once Young Albert was settled at his table, Suki sitting next to him in her wheelchair, the Landlady made an announcement. Everyone in the pub was looking their way anyhow.

"Everyone," she said. "You all know Young Albert and I'd like to introduce his new friend, all the way from Japan, Miss Suki."

Well the customers, a mixture of old, middle-aged and young couples out to enjoy lunch and young men gathered around the bar, couldn't help but to clap politely and nod and smile in Young Albert's direction.

Young Albert nodded, smiled back then took hold of Suki's hand. He felt chuffed and could tell that Suki felt the same way too.

"Brown Fillup is it then?" the Landlady asked, getting down to business.

"Er... Yes and can you put the brown ale in a glass this time?"

"For Miss Suki, yes of course... and lunch?"

Young Albert rubbed his chin, "I think the steak and kidney pie and chips would be very nice," he said. "Just the one plate as me and Suki will share."

"Of course," said the Landlady courteously.

With that, she went to attend to her business leaving Young Albert feeling kind of exposed, what with every pair of eyes in the bar being on him and Suki. Finally, one of the younger men spoke up. He was sitting on a high stool at the corner of the bar closest to them.

"From Japan you say, Mister Albert?"

"Aye lad! Tokyo."

After a quick swig of his pint of ale the young man, half off the stool already, asked, "Mind if I come over to meet her? My name's Tom, by the way."

"Not at all er... Tom," Young Albert said... politely but, not being used to such attention, with some reticence.

The young man though wasted no time and, on his arrival at Young Albert's table, pulled out a chair and sat down. "Amazing," he said, staring at Suki. "Absolutely amazing."

"Yes, it is a long way," Young Albert said, somewhat pointedly. He gave the young man a meaningful look. "But what with modern air travel..."

Meanwhile the Landlady was smiling to herself. She had had a feeling that Miss Suki was going to be good for business and so she proved to be... good for business and good for Young Albert.

During that lunchtime he and Suki were never short of company and, what's more, Young Albert never had to pay for one drop of ale.

It seemed as well that word must have gotten around as within half-an-hour of his and Suki's arrival the pub was packed.

After the steak and kidney pie and chips and four or five Brown Fillups, Young Albert decided that it was time to head for home.

"Cheers, Young Albert... Miss Suki," the old, the middle-aged and the young couples called as he and Suki left.

"See you again, Miss Suki... Mister Albert," said the young men gathered around the bar.

"Don't be a stranger now," the Landlady called out. "Always a warm welcome for you and Miss Suki here."

A few minutes after they had left, unnoticed and unseen, the mousey-looking woman, this time accompanied by her even mousier-looking husband, scurried out from the opposite side of the bar and scuttled as fast as they could up the street.

The Parable of Young Albert
Chapter Eight
Homeward Bound

Well, as previously mentioned, Young Albert had supped four or five Brown Fillups during the course of lunch and, only being used to the one quiet pint of an afternoon, well… well it's a good job that he had Suki's wheelchair to hold onto, let's put it that way.

By now, it was three o' clock of a Sunday afternoon and chintz curtains were rustling with gay abandon. As he and Suki made their way, the chintz curtains created a ripple-effect reminiscent of a ship's bow wave preceding them up the street.

So then as Young Albert and his Oriental charge made their meandering way home, the chintz curtains were flapping furiously with whisperings and mutterings behind them.

"Well I never did!"

"So that's the Chinese Girl?"

"Japanese, our Phyllis, Japanese."

Then, the voice of a child, "Why can't Mister Albert's girlfriend walk, mam?" Followed by, "Shush!"

Of course, Young Albert was oblivious to all this and, even if he had been privy to the whisperings, he had enough of a job to navigate his way home to have been worried about it.

All this being so, Young Albert was in a blissful mood as he and Suki meandered up their front path and into the house.

Immediately they were inside, he helped Suki out of her wheelchair, took the jacket from around her shoulders and helped her to get settled into her armchair by the fireplace.

As he put the English wool blanket back over her knees, he kissed her on the forehead again and closed her eyes.

"I think we both could do with a nap after all that," he said, flopping down in his own armchair.

It felt to Young Albert as he had only just closed his eyes when a loud pounding on the front door, followed by a shrill, ululating cacophony, jerked him awake.

"Come on, you pervert! We know you're in there. You and that trollop doll of yours."

Tiredly, Young Albert got to his feet and went to the door.

"What's all…?"

Before he could even finish off his query, the 'Meals on Wheels' lady cut him off.

"We've heard about you," she yipped.

"Perverting the youth of the village," the School Ma'am yapped.

"And on a Good Sunday an' all," the Head Postmistress yelped. "Have you no shame?"

"Corrupting the young!"

"On the Sabbath an' all."

They were, of course, by no means finished when Young Albert, still in an intoxicated haze, quietly closed the door.

"Don't think you've seen the last of us, you degenerate deviant!" they shrieked as the door closed in their faces. "We'll be back!"

Giving up for now, nodding their heads and clucking, the 'Three Banshees' headed back down the front path. However, the Head Postmistress scuttled back, bent down by the front door and howled through the flap of the letterbox. "I'm writing to your sister in Manchester," she wailed. "She'll put a spanner in your works she will!"

The Parable of Young Albert
Chapter Nine
Sister Margaret

Monday to Wednesday there were no further demonstrations. Although ominous in itself, Young Albert and Suki welcomed this respite. It gave Suki the chance to join Young Albert on his morning walks and, of course, to join him in his lunchtime Brown Fillup, the Landlady at the 'Den of Inik Witty' doing a better than normal trade at the same time.

However, first thing Thursday morning, after driving through the night, Young Albert's sister was on his doorstep… and she looked vexed.

"Our Margaret!" Young Albert said, opening the door still in his pyjamas.

"Don't you 'Our Margaret' me," his sister replied, pushing past him. "Where is she?"

"If you mean Suki, she's still in bed."

"How could you, Our Albert?" she said, taking her coat off. "Taking up with a trollop, an harlot of the eventide and you a man of your age."

"Better sit down, Our Margaret," Young Albert said. "It's not what you think. I'll make us a nice cup of tea."

While the tea was brewing, and Sister Margaret was mulling over what she had just heard, Young Albert went to Suki's bedroom and, gently, woke her up.

"Good morning, Suki," he said. "We've an unexpected visitor."

"Here she is," he said, getting Suki settled into her place at the table. "Our Margaret, this is Suki."

"Well!" she said. "Not what that harpy at the post office led me to believe at all."

"No, I imagine not," said Young Albert, pouring the tea.

Young Albert's sister Margaret managed, over the next three days, to convince him of the sensible thing to do.

She told him repeatedly on their morning walks that, unless something changed, the 'Three Harpies' (no matter how many times Young Albert reminded her that they were in fact 'Banshees') would be back at it threefold once she went back to Manchester. There was, Sister Margaret said, only one thing to be done.

Well, Young Albert, bowing to her wisdom, finally agreed… provided that is that she stayed until Monday.

To this, Sister Margaret readily agreed and so Sunday morning saw the three of them heading to the 'Den of Inik Witty' for Sunday lunch.

Well, let me tell you, the entire village and half of Turn had learned of the imminent departure of Miss Suki. When they got there the pub was packed to such an extent… even the twitchers of the chintz curtains, out of curiosity, were in attendance… that the Landlady had to blaze a trail to enable them to get to Young Albert's usual table.

"We'll miss you, Miss Suki!" the customers said as the threesome worked their way through.

"Brown Fillup, Mister Albert? One for your sister?" called the young man who had first sat with them the Sunday before.

"It's a bloody crying shame!" his mate blurted out, having had one over the odds already.

Yes, the locals were none too pleased at this turn of events. Even the mousey-looking lady and her even mousier-looking husband sent word that they regretted it had come to this.

Of course, the 'Three Bloody Banshees' weren't there. They had won and, after the courier had been tomorrow, that scandalous Young Albert

could just stay home on his Jack Jones, wait for his meals on wheels and learn how to be respectable and it was no use of him coming crying to them. Needless to say, those three meddling buggars were not missed.

A Sunday lunch of steak and kidney pie, chips and peas was laid on for Young Albert and his sister (Miss Suki sharing with Young Albert) by the Landlady at no charge. Meanwhile, neither Young Albert nor his sister paid a brass penny for the Brown Fillups that they downed… and they downed a large quantity. In fact, everyone present overdid things somewhat during that Sunday lunch and the Landlady shed a quiet tear when, at three in the afternoon, Young Albert, his sister and Miss Suki worked their way to the door… Young Albert and his sister having a firm grasp of Miss Suki's wheelchair.

The Parable of Young Albert
Chapter Ten
The Sensible Thing

The details of Miss Suki's departure had been explained at some length during the Sunday lunch.

On the Monday morning, bright and early, Young Albert's sister would be setting off back to Manchester. Young Albert would then get Miss Suki packed and ready for the courier's noon-time run. She would be going back whence she came… 'Akihabara Doll Works, Tokyo, Japan'.

No, Young Albert would not give in to the entreaties of the young men offering to make room for her at their house. Nor would he, regrettably, agree to the Landlady's proposition that, for room and board, she come to work for her. This latter proposition, Young Albert said, would just be too upsetting for him. The only thing he could think of was to stick to what was sensible.

Needless to say, Sunday night was a sleepless night for Young Albert. He fancied that Suki had not slept much either and, during the course of breakfast, no-one either said or ate much.

As he sat, staring into the bottom of his teacup, Young Albert was aware of the clock ticking away the minutes and he knew, try to delay the inevitable though he might, his sister would soon be heading back to her home up North. Her suitcase and handbag were already standing by the door and she had already finished her cup of tea.

"Come on then," Margaret said as she got to her feet. "I've a long journey and I don't think as you'll be wanting me here when you say goodbye to Miss Suki."

At this, Young Albert dabbed tears from his eyes. "Well," he sniffled. "You must think as I am a soft old buggar."

"Come on now, Our Albert," she said, putting a hand comfortingly on his shoulder. "I know as you need some company but there must be a local woman as takes your eye?"

Without replying, Young Albert got to his feet. "I'll be alright, Our Margaret," he said stoutly. "Don't you worry about me."

"I know you will, Our Albert. And you see that you look after yourself," his sister said, heading for the door.

As she loaded up her suitcase into the boot of her car, the 'Three Banshees', perched on the low wall of a neighbour's garden, glared at her balefully.

A shiver ran up her spine as she got into the car and drove away. Young Albert watched her go, then closed the door and went back inside.

The Parable of Young Albert
Chapter Eleven
'Nil Illigitimi Carborundum'

Once back in the house, Young Albert stood looking at Suki. She sat, hands resting against the edge of the breakfast table, just as he had taught her when she had first arrived on his birthday.

"Come on, Suki," he said, with sudden resolve, helping her out of her seat and into the wheelchair. "Time for our morning walk."

Young Albert had, of course, made his own mind up about the sensible thing to do… and it did not involve sending Miss Suki back to Japan, or anywhere else for that matter.

He had noticed that there was a fresh wind blowing when he had seen their Margaret off so, after putting on his customary tweed jacket and cap, he put his old sports jacket around Suki's shoulders and the English wool blanket over her legs.

"It's a bit nippy out this morning, Suki," he said as he manoeuvred her wheelchair out the door. "Nice and fresh though," he added, closing the door resolutely.

Ie held his head high and he could see that Miss Suki was holding her head high too, as they set off down the front path and onto the street.

"Taking Miss Suki out for one last walk, Young Albert?" the 'Three Banshees' called out, in a somewhat mocking tone I might add.

"Fuck you!" Young Albert replied pleasantly and, without even looking back, carried on up the street.

Well, apart from an astonished, "Well I never!" the 'Three Banshees' never bothered Young Albert and Miss Suki ever again.

So ever after that day, Young Albert and Miss Suki led their best life. Miss Suki would always accompany Young Albert on his early morning walks, come wind, rain or shine. He would always take her to the pub with him at lunchtime where she shared in his Brown Fillup and pie and chips. The Landlady, of course, was always happy to see them and their Sunday Dinner on the house became a matter of course.

Many a night they would sit by the fireside, Young Albert either reading to Miss Suki from the newspaper or his latest library book. Spinning yarns of days of old was also a favourite pastime for both of them, or maybe even having a bit of a nap after supper.

On fine evenings in the warmer weather, they would sit out in the backyard on an old garden bench that Constable Howard had brought round for them. Whether this was meant in some way to compensate for the rough handling his Great Aunt and her friends had dealt out to him and Miss Suki, Young Albert neither knew nor did he care. Despite the antics of his Great Aunt, Constable Howard was a good, solid sort and so the old garden bench was accepted with good grace.

Despite, over a period of time, Miss Suki's bedroom being made even more comfortable for her, what with a new duvet, matching curtains and even a dressing table with hairbrush and cosmetics, there were times when she shared Young Albert's bed… but only on the very coldest nights in the deepest of deep mid-winter.

An Adventure Down the Chippy

Written by Lynne Preston

BOSTOCK HOUSE PUBLISHING

ESTABLISHED 2025

A Story from the Golden Age of the 1960's

During the Mid 'Sixties, in Great Britain, there arose two rival youth groups. On the one hand, the Rockers rode motorbikes, wore leather jackets and, in some cases, rode around terrorising the towns. The type of motorbike was much as described in this short tale, with five a gallon fuel tank, handlebars that clipped onto the upper part of the front suspension and rear set footrests. The more chrome the merrier and, instead of a silencer or muffler, they favoured a megaphone, known as a Mega, attached to the end of the exhaust pipe. This type of motorcycle in this modern age is known as a Café Racer. One ambition of a good rocker was to get the bike to do the 'Ton'... a hundred miles per hour. The accuracy of speedometers in those days meaning that when the clock did indicate the Ton, you were more likely doing a good eighty or ninety miles an hour.

On the other hand the Mods wore the most up to date clobber, the ultimate being from the boutiques of Leicester Square and Carnaby Street. Their transport of choice was the scooter, mostly Lambretta's with a smattering of Vespa's. They could never get enough mirrors and spotlights on their machines and a favourite seat cover was the type that featured the Union Flag, perhaps bearing a likeness of King Edward VII. A whip aerial with pennant was also de rigueur. They were more interested in style rather than speed, although the Lambretta SX250 was reputed to pack a punch.

This story then, although fiction, is meant as a window into that bygone age.

An Adventure Down the Chippy
Lynne Preston

Table of Contents

Cast of Characters

Brother Judd	The Rocker
Bazza	The Mod
Little Miss Never You Mind	The Mod Girl
Our Ethel	The First Chippy Lady
Our Mavis	Our Ethel's Cousin

An Adventure Down the Chippy
Chapter One
The Rocker

One hot August day in 1964, a Rocker barrels like the clappers down Nantwich Road. His Triumph Thunderbird thunders along beneath him, eating up the miles. A glance at the clock, a grin of satisfaction… the ton… with ease.

He cracks on, sweeping round the esses and under the aqueduct, easing up on the throttle as he enters the outskirts of Middlewich to bring the bike down to thirty miles an hour. The cops can't catch him at speed… or, at least, they never have… and getting copped for thirty-five miles an hour in a built-up area would hold no glory.

So, he eases back, lets go of the clip-on handlebars, sits up, pulls a comb from a top pocket of his leather jacket, combs back his thick black hair… the Thunderbird now just ambling along… leans forward and checks the results of his work in the chrome handlebar mirror.

Satisfied, the Rocker returns the comb to the pocket, drops down over the five-gallon polished aluminium tank and grips, once more, the clip-on bars.

As he enters the town proper, he goes down through the gears to ease onto Wheelock Street then, a few yards up the road, pulls over into Lawrence Avenue. Every house at this end of the avenue has a low wall to separate the garden from the road. He brings the bike to a stop and pulls it onto its centre stand in front of one of these walls. There is a chip shop cafe on Wheelock Street only a few yards from here so, at a swaggering gait, the Rocker strides, leather motorbike boots creaking nicely, in that direction.

He had noticed, could not help but to notice, a lone Mod scooter parked just up the avenue from where the Thunderbird stands.

The Rocker nods in satisfaction. He recognises the scooter; "Belongs to that little twat, Bazza," he mutters as he strides along.

As he turns the corner onto Wheelock Street, one of the locals hurriedly steps off the pavement to get out of his way.

Another local, beyond the Rocker's actual destination, sees him, looks right, left, then right again and trots across to the other side of the road.

The Rocker pays no heed to any of these antics… in fact he doesn't even notice… he is too intent on the promise of pie and chips with mushy peas… and cornering the lone Mod.

An Adventure Down the Chippy
Chapter Two
Fish 'n' Chips Twice

Pushing the door aside, the Rocker strides into the chippy. Customers, already at the counter, turn to look... but not too intently. As he swaggers through, metal motorbike badges glint from the front of his leather jacket and, on the back, silver studs spell out the menacing words, 'The Brothers Grim'.

One of the ladies behind the counter, salt-stained chip-fat apron with a whiff of malt vinegar draped over her, remarks, in the voice of a scold and with a clucking of tongue, "Just look at that, our Mavis. The Brothers Grim if you please. What the world is coming to I don't know, I don't."

"Nor me, our Ethel," replies her colleague in much the same tone. She dips her scoop into the chip pan. "Nor me!" With this, they both dismiss the lout from their minds and go back to the business of filling chip bags.

Meanwhile, the Rocker has entered the café at the back of the chippy and has spotted his erstwhile quarry sitting at a corner table. Unexpectedly though, he sees he is not on his Jack Jones. Oh no, indeed not! Rather, at his side, sits a rather scrumptious looking Mod Girl.

"Bloody 'ell!" thinks the Rocker, instantly adjusting his demeanour and lengthening his stride in their direction. "Bloody, bloody 'ell."

"Nar then, Bazza ya little twat!" he quips jovially, turning a chair around at their table to straddle himself across it. "What's this yuv got with ya?" He tips his head towards the girl, brows furrowed an with an expectant look on his face. "Does her mother know she's out?"

"'This,'" replies the Mod (somewhat indignantly I might add). "Is a young lady... and she happens to have a name."

"Well," says the Rocker, getting to his feet and making a theatrical motion as if to sweep a non-existent hat from his head... at the same time bowing. "Pardon my manners for the ignorant reptile that I am."

Just as suddenly as he got to his feet, he once again plonks himself down... once again straddling the chair.

This time he turns to the Mod Girl... dirty-blonde hair cut pixie style as in the latest Twiggy fashion... black and white checkered dress, matching handbag on the small table. Figure, unlike Twiggy's, possessing some pleasing curves.

He nods, politely. "Brother Judd," he says, by way of introduction. "And your name, Miss," he asks, using his best Sunday School manners.

"Never-You-Mind," she retorts. "That's what my name is," (and this time with much more emphasis) "Never-You-Mind!"

Somewhat taken aback the Rocker addresses the Mod, "How did you meet her then?" he demands abruptly. "Little-Miss-Never-You-Mind here."

However, it is the Mod Girl that replies. "He met me outside Marks and Sparks if you must know," she says, somewhat testily.

"What? In Sandbach?"

"Yes, in Sandbach," the Mod cuts in. "What of it?"

Before the Rocker can say what it is it will be of, Our Ethel comes through from the front.

"Now then you lot," she says, giving them all the fish-eye. "Keep it down! I've got decent customers as want seeing to up front so I have." Her statement not being challenged by the young buggars she asks, in the shrill voice required of chippy ladies of the time, "Do you want summat eat? Or have you just come in here to spoil me day?"

Somewhat quelled by this matronly figure (perhaps she reminds him of his Mam... but I cannot say for sure) it is the Rocker that replies first,

again using his best Sunday School manners, "I'll have steak and kidney pie, chips, mushy peas, a big pickled onion, a couple o' slabs o' bread 'n' butter and a cold Coke." Then, after a pause, "Please."

(At this point I feel compelled to inform the gentle reader that, during this golden age of the 'Sixties, cholesterol had yet to be invented, fridges were at a premium and if you wanted a cold drink of any sort, you had to be specific about it).

"And you two?" the Chippy Lady shrills having committed the Rocker's order to memory.

"Oh, er..." stammers the Mod.

"We'll have fish and chips twice," the Mod Girl butts in. "And a pot of tea."

The Chippy Lady turns in the direction of the serving hatch. "Steak and kidney pie, chips, mushy peas, a big pickled onion, a couple o' slabs o' bread 'n' butter a cold Coke, fish 'n' chips twice and a pot o' tea," she shrieks. Then, as an amendment, "Pot o' tea fer two!"

"Alright, I heard you the first time!" her cohort yells.

With that, and an admonishment to the young buggars to behave, Our Ethel bustles off back to the front of the chippy.

"Right then!" the Rocker says, turning to face the Mod the minute the Chippy Lady was back out the door. "I owe you a bloody good hidin'."

The Mod girl looks from one to the other, then square-on she faces the Rocker. "A bloody good hidin'?" She looks the Rocker up and down. Then, somewhat protectively, "What's he ever done to you?"

"What's his bloody mates done more like!" the Rocker replies defiantly.

At this point, the Mod jumps in with, "I've told ya, they weren't my mates." Belligerently, he smacks a closed fist down on the table, causing the vinegar bottle (such as every chippy had in those days) to skip a merry dance.

Seeing this, the Rocker jumps to his feet, starts to peel off his leather jacket. "Right then!" he says, eyes focused intently on the Mod. "Let's get at it."

His deliberations are interrupted by a shrill shriek, "There'll be none o' that in 'ere!" then, "Bloody lads!"

The Rocker turns to see the Chippy Lady's head poking through the serving hatch. He shrugs his leather jacket back onto his shoulders; the Mod eases back into his seat. The Mod Girl sighs with relief.

An Adventure Down the Chippy
Chapter Three
Like Two Spoiled Schoolboys

Neither the Rocker, nor the Mod will look at each other, the one staring up at the ceiling, the other gazing down at the floor.

The Mod girl, once more, looks from one to the other, lets out a deep sigh. "Just look at you pair," she says. "Like a pair of spoiled schoolboys."

The Rocker comes back to Earth; the Mod raises his gaze.

"Tell you what," says the Rocker, filled now with a kind of wild enthusiasm. "I'll make you a deal."

"Oh?" says the Mod, somewhat cautiously.

"Yes," says the Rocker, eyeing the Mod intently. "I'll pay for your dinner, the pair of you… and the pot of tea, dinner on me, all three of us, if…"

"Sounds a bit too good to be true," the Mod interrupts.

"That's not all!" the Rocker, continues, unwilling to give up the floor.

"It isn't?" the Mod, once again interjecting and in a rather squeaky voice at that, says.

"No, not by half," a pause and then, "If you stand down and let me take Little-Miss-Never-You-Mind here to Prestatyn for a day out you get all that and I won't even duff you up."

Well, the Mod Girl was red-faced outraged… beside herself with anger.

"Take me to bloody Prestatyn and you won't even duff him up?" she yells, starting to get out of her seat.

"Well yeah! Unless you'd sooner go Blackpool?"

"Sooner go Blackpool? Sooner go Blackpool?" She grabs hold of her handbag and starts to swing. Again that shrill shrieking voice, "When you lot have finished your argy-bargy, your dinner's ready… and it isn't goin' grow legs and come to you." The Mod attempts to hold the Mod Girl back by sweeping an outstretched arm in front of her; the Mod Girl, contemptuous, slaps it aside, smacks the Rocker over the head with her checkered handbag. The Rocker lets out a bit of a yelp, rubs his head, gets to his feet and, still rubbing his head, swaggers over to the serving hatch.

"That'll be three 'n' six!" the chippy lady screeches, looking in some degree of expectation at the Rocker.

"Three-and-a-bloody-kick?" the Rocker retorts, eyeing up the contents of the proffered tray. "I'd only aff pay three bob fer that lot in Nantwich."

The Chippy Lady, without relinquishing her grip on the aforementioned tray, shrieks, over her shoulder, "Mavis!" to a squawked rejoinder of, "What?"

"I don't know what we're goin' do with all this. This soft buggar says they're goin' go Nantwich instead."

Just then, the Mod Girl shoves the Rocker aside. "Nobody is going go Nantwich," she says calmly, at the same time as giving the Rocker a look. "This twerp was just about to hand over his three-and-a-kick… Unless he wants another lamping from my handbag?"

With that, the Mod Girl takes hold of the tray, the Chippy Lady relinquishes her grip and the Rocker fumbles about in his pockets for the much-fabled three-and-a-kick*.

*Three and a kick is three shillings and sixpence… Three 'n' six… A kick being slang for a tanner, a sixpenny piece. Three bob is three shillings.

An Adventure Down the Chippy
Chapter Four
Pie and Chips Butty

Things having settled down somewhat, the three of them dig into their dinners.

The Rocker, relatively unphased by the lamping he'd had, grabs up a slab of the thick white bread… it is thickly coated with butter. In fact, Middlewich being situated in dairy country, both slabs are thickly coated in butter. With the one slab balanced on the palm of one hand, he arranges as many chips as he can on its surface. Satisfied with his artwork, he then cuts off half of the steak and kidney pie and, by much prodding and poking with his fork (which the Mod Girl is surprised to see him use) manages to get it on top of the chips. Then, mushy peas plastered all over the top of the pie, the coup-de-grace… the big pickled onion. The Mod girl rolls her eyes as the Rocker slaps the second slab of thick white bread on top of all this and compresses it between his hands. Then, still using both hands, takes a bloody great bite. As he leans back, chewing and mumbling, a look of ecstasy comes over his face.

"It's only a bloody chip butty," the Mod Girl says. "You'd think it was that fillet steak me dad keeps goin' on about."

The Rocker though is unphased. He knows good food when he sees it… knows how to bloody well enjoy it as well.

Chip butty eaten, the Rocker gargles a gulp of cold Coke down his throat, utters something like, "BAH!" then sets to on the rest of his dinner with his knife and fork which, once again, the Mod Girl is surprised to see him use.

"Have you thought about it then," he says between chews, eyeing the Mod Girl.

"Thought about what?" she replies, somewhat snappily and knowing full well what he was on about.

"The day out... Prestatyn? Blackpool? Maybe somewhere a bit posher?"

At this point, the Mod buts in. "Hoi!" he barks, stabbing at his chips with his fork. "I've not said yes yet."

The Rocker shrugs and bends his head back to his pie and chips; the Mod Girl just shakes her head, but decides to keep mum until after she's enjoyed the free dinner.

An Adventure Down the Chippy
Chapter Five
The Mod Girl Strikes Back

The Rocker pushes his now empty plate away from him, sits upright and squares his shoulders. "Now then!" he says, looking the Mod square in the face. "Let's have it! Yer answer."

Before the Mod can even open his mouth, the Mod Girl is on her feet, picks the teapot up and empties the dregs on the Mod's head, the teapot lid giving him a smart smack to boot.

"What the bloody 'ell?" He leaps to his feet, shoving the table over as he does so. The Rocker, not being inclined to be sent sprawling by the force of the table against the back of his chair, rapidly follows suit.

"Have you gone knocked?" the Mod gasps, dregs of tea dripping from his hitherto nicely styled hair. "What did I do?"

"See if you can work it out for yourself!"

She sweeps her handbag up off the floor, the Rocker shies back and the Mod Girl stamps off towards the door.

"What the bloody 'ell?" the Mod says.

"Beats me." Then, together (in exasperation) "Women!"

"You young buggars," the Chippy Lady howls, her head thrust through the serving hatch. "I told you behave. Now look at it. Mavis already went home with headache and now look at all this mess I've to clean up."

"Well, I'm… I'm…" the Rocker mutters, using his best Sunday School manners. He takes hold of the upturned table.

It is the Mod, however, who, having been to Grammar School, is the first to recover his equilibrium.

"Madam," he says gallantly, patting his tea-soaked hair about with his hands. "My fault entirely. Please allow me and my mate here to assist you in your endeavours to restore this handsome little café to its former pristine glory."

Well, needless to say, this little speech takes the Chippy Lady somewhat aback. Not knowing quite what to make of it, but not wanting to tip them out if they are going to prove useful, she agrees to the compromise.

"Alright," she says. She jerks her head to the far and opposite corner of the room. "You'll find a mop 'n' bucket over yonder. And don't take all day. My hubby's home by now waiting take me Crewe Market."

An Adventure Down the Chippy
Chapter Six
A Job Well Done

Job done and the two now having made some sort of uneasy alliance, the Mod and the Rocker alight the stone steps of the Chippy. Cirrus clouds form wispy mare's tails across the lofty blue sky; the strains of 'House of the Rising Sun' waft on the breeze… emanating from a tinny transistor radio in a Lawrence Avenue backyard perhaps?

However, more immediately to hand is a Crosville Double-Decker bus, just pulling away from the curb and bound for Sandbach.

The Mod girl is in the front seat, upper saloon of the bus. She bangs on the window with her handbag; the Mod and the Rocker look up. The Mod Girl waves, smiles, then, without further ado, gives them the two-fingered salute.

"Charmin'", the Rocker remarks, as the double-decker slowly gains momentum.

"Met her this morning, so I did," says the Mod, reflectively. "Riding me scooter and minding me own business when she flagged me down."

"Ah, yes!" quoth the Rocker, tongue in cheek. "I know how that can be."

"Ah, well!" the Mod sighs. "There's bound be more fish in the sea."

"Ah! Waiting fer thee outside Marks and Sparks I shudna wonder." He slaps the Mod on the back. "Come on, I'll thrash thee at darts down th' 'Red Lion'."

Epilogue

As the years rolled by and the 'Sixties slowly gave way to the 'Seventies; the 'Seventies inevitably giving way to the 'Eighties, the trio, of course, were making their own way in life.

The Mod Girl had been especially successful in that by the time she was thirty she was already managing not one, but three of Marks and Sparks department stores and although two of them were most prestigious... one in Chester and the other in Manchester, she still kept hold of the one in Sandbach, that particular one holding some very fond personal memories. Yes, she is married, yes, she has a family and yes, her husband is neither a Mod nor indeed a Rocker.

The Mod himself? Well, even a Mod can get lucky. He met his future wife, another Mod Girl, at Robin Hood Camp in Prestatyn, of all places, the following summer. They had been renting caravans with their mates; the Mod Girl having arrived in a Mini-Cooper along with five other girls. The Mod there with likewise fellows, all with Lambretta scooters festooned with chrome lights and mirrors. The Mod and the Mod Mini-Cooper Girl had fallen in love right there and then and, when the time came, they invited the Rocker to the wedding so they did. The Rocker even brought them gifts, a new whip aerial for his scooter and a leather steering wheel cover for her Mini-Cooper. At the same time the original Mod Girl from the Chippy had been invited by the Mod's fiancée, they having been friends for many years.

Although awkward at first, the Mod schooled the Rocker on what had worked for him... which enabled the Rocker to make amends at last. Ah, yes! So, the Mod then is all settled down and doing well by his wife and family. He works, incidentally, at a wagon works not all that far from the 'Marks and Sparks'.

Now, the Rocker... Ah yes... the Rocker. Not long after the Mod's wedding and his making up (so to speak) with the Mod Girl from down the Chippy, he had an epiphany. This being so and after first consulting with his local pastor, he took the pre-requisite courses, performed the required work experience and took ship to Africa where he became, and still is to this day, a missionary and founder member of many charities and thus truly deserving of the title Brother Judd.

The Weary Traveller

Written by Lynne Preston

BOSTOCK HOUSE PUBLISHING

ESTABLISHED 2025

Introduction

The idea of the weary traveller and his outlandish garb occurred to me from one of my own adventures long ago in which I arrived back from Morocco wearing a sombrero, kaftan and a pair of beaten up old sandals.

However, the rest of this story is a fanciful tale, intended for the purposes of entertainment only and not intended in any way to reflect upon the hardworking staff and officials at the airports of the world or the weary travellers who journey there through.

The Weary Traveller

Written by Lynne Preston

Cast of Characters

The Customs Official

The Weary Traveller

The Jobsworth

The Bloody Great Bobby

The Two Neatly Mustachioed Gentlemen

The Weary Traveller
Somewhen in the Late Twentieth Century

A gentleman in neat business attire, leather briefcase clasped in one hand, neat mustachioed features bearing a business-like smile, approaches the Customs and Immigration Official and presents his passport. The official takes the passport, opens it, mutters, "Hello… Hello… Hello?" whisks away the slim plain brown envelope secreted therein and slips it into his arse pocket where it nestles comfortably with another similar, albeit rather exotically styled, envelope of the same ilk.

"Reason for your visit, sir?" he asks, in a perfunctory fashion.

"Business, I guess," the neat mustachioed gentleman replies.

"Then business I guess it is!" The Customs Official's stamp comes down with an officious thwack on the relevant page of the passport. He hands it back to the neat mustachioed gentleman. "You'll find the lift up to the VIP Complimentary Shuttle Lounge just down the hall, Sir."

With a nod and a thank you the gentleman takes his leather briefcase and his neat mustachioed features down the hall as indicated by the very co-operative Customs Official.

The Customs Official gives his arse pocket a smart smack and looks up to see who is next.

"Hello… Hello… Hello?" he mutters again, but in a much different tone, as a man in ridiculous Bermuda shorts, waist-length kaftan and sombrero approaches. The Customs Official glances down to see he is also wearing an abominable pair of flip-flops. Far from sporting neat mustachioed features, this man is red-faced and sweating like an old bull. With an old duffle bag, two bulging suitcases and a hearty, "Ole!" the man steams up to the counter.

"Ole! Is it?" the Customs Official snaps. "Where've you been? What's in the bags?" Before the very obvious holiday-maker can reply, his passport and tatty old wallet slip from under his arm.

"What?" says the Customs Official, eyeing the tatty old wallet. "Attempting to bribe an Officer in the Service of Her Majesty the Queen is it?"

A security man, having observed the proceedings (and seeing his chance to do his jobsworth) scuttles up to the scene.

He quickly consults the Customs Official. "Strip search, sir?" he pants, brow furrowed and hopeful.

"Strip search!" the Customs Official replies crisply. "And secure the evidence from the floor."

"But I…" The heretofore hearty traveller gets no further. He feels a heavy hand lay hold of his kaftan collar.

The heretofore hearty traveller, still sweating like an old bull, looks over his shoulder to see a Bloody Great Bobby glaring at him.

"Been abroad 'ave we, sir?" the Bloody Great Bobby says portentously. "And now attempting to bribe an Officer in the Service of Her Majesty the Queen? Very serious offence that, my lad… very serious! Now then… Let's be 'avin' you!"

The Bloody Great Bobby and Mister Jobsworth, with the officious Customs Official trotting behind, quick-march him to a small windowless room overlooked, as indeed was the entire Customs Hall, by the panoramic glass panes of the VIP Complimentary Shuttle Lounge.

Behind these rather magnificent panes, the neatly-mustachioed gentleman featured earlier stands, one hand holding a dainty saucer, the other hand (pinky extended) holding the dainty handle of a dainty cup. He sips casually at the complimentary cup of tea. He turns to another neatly-mustachioed gentleman (this neatly-mustachioed gentleman being in possession of rather swarthy features) that stands nearby.

"Tut-tut-tut," he says, with a shake of his neatly styled head (word has travelled fast). "Imagine attempting to offer an Officer in the Service of Her Majesty the Queen a bribe?"

"In broad daylight as well," replies the neatly-mustachioed gentleman possessing the rather swarthy features.

"Tut! Tut! Tut!" they repeat between sips of their complimentary dainty cups of tea. "Tut! Tut! Tut!"

Meanwhile, the heretofore hearty but now worn to a ravelling traveller is by now sans-clobber in the strip-search room. The contents of his bulging suitcases are strewn all over the floor and the little jobsworth is in the process of emptying out his old duffle bag onto a table.

"Very serious this!" repeats the Bloody Great Bobby. "Very, very serious."

"Very serious indeed," affirms the Customs Official. "Very serious indeed!"

As the jobsworth is rooting through the contents of the heretofore hearty but now worn to a ravelling traveller's old duffle bag; souvenirs and trinkets from every foreign port imaginable, crumpled, well-thumbed photos of rather dubious-looking ladies and every conceivable bit of tit-tat a traveller of his ilk is liable to pick up, the Customs Official is taking a very keen interest in the tattered old wallet. He looks at it thoughtfully, weighs it in his hand, opens it, has a quick butcher's at the contents. Notes, notes, notes! Nothing but banknotes. He has a crafty shufty round the room. The Bloody Great Bobby is studying the floor, kicking the strewn contents of the suitcases around; the jobsworth is pouring over the heretofore hearty but now worn to a ravelling traveller's belongings spread over the table. The heretofore hearty but now worn to a ravelling traveller himself is bent over, attempting to cover his sensitive parts with his hands.

Seeing that he is not observed, the Customs Official rifles through the notes. Euros, Dirhams, Ryals… all adding up to a tidy sum… a very tidy sum… a very tidy sum indeed. And what's this? Canadian dollars?"

He tucks the notes back into the tattered old wallet. "Ahem!" says he, attracting the attention of the Bloody Great Bobby and the squirrelly little runt of a jobsworth. "I think," says he, slipping the tattered old wallet into his inside pocket. "I think that there has been a mistake."

The squirrelly little runt of a jobsworth looks up from his jobsworth of a job questioningly. The Bloody Great Bobby lifts his head and says, "What have we here then?"

"A mistake," the Customs Official repeats. "This man has merely lost his wallet."

The heretofore hearty but now worn to a ravelling traveller looks, open-mouthed, at the Customs Official.

"But," says he. "I haven't…"

At this point, the squirrelly little runt of a jobsworth chimes in, "But he," he says, pointing an accusing finger at the heretofore hearty but now worn to a ravelling traveller, "but he attempted to bribe you and dropped his wallet in his haste."

"Nonsense!" the Customs Official asserts. "Balderdash! How can the poor man have 'Dropped his wallet in his haste' when he has already lost that very same wallet?" He pauses, brow furrowed, chin clasped in one hand. "No… Probably stolen by some knave in one of those foreign ports one hears of!"

"But…?"

"Silence," the Customs Official snaps, taking back command of the situation. "Constable, I'm sure you have better things to do." He looks meaningfully at the Bloody Great Bobby. "I need detain you no further." He switches his attention back to the squirrelly little runt of a jobsworth, "And you," he says. "What do you think you are doing going through this weary traveller's belongings? Off you go and harass an old lady, or whatever it is you are good at."

Seeing nothing else for it, the squirrelly little runt of a jobsworth makes haste to exit the room. The Bloody Great Bobby, with a muttered, "Evenin' all!" plods off behind him.

"Now then, my man," the Customs Official says, looking the heretofore hearty but now worn to a ravelling traveller up and down. "Get your clobber back on and gather up your things."

The heretofore hearty but now worn to a ravelling traveller, with a stunned look on his face, scoops his underdrawers up off the floor. He hops around on one leg in his haste to get them on.

"Ah, yes!" says the Customs Official pointedly whilst feeling the bulk of the tatty old wallet not-so-secretly-secreted in his inside pocket. "I say as it's a shame that you have lost your wallet," he goes on, in a rather raised voice. "A great shame… however, I dare say that such are the risks of international travel."

"But?" says the heretofore hearty but now worn to a ravelling traveller incredulously, while pulling up his ridiculous Bermuda shorts. "I haven't lost my wallet."

"What? Haven't lost your wallet?" The Customs Official makes to open the door of the strip-search room. "Lying to the police is it? Very serious offence that, let alone lying to an Officer in the Service of Her Majesty the Queen. Hmm? I don't think that the Old Bill will take very kindly to this series of events I don't. First claiming to have lost your wallet then making contrary assertations."

"But I…" the heretofore hearty but now worn to a ravelling traveller pulls his Kaftan over his head. It feels damp to his skin, but still he is grateful for it and so settles it into place.

"But you what?" enquires the Customs Official, looking him in the eye, one hand on the door knob. "Attempted to bribe an officer in the Service of Her Majesty the Queen?"

Slipping his feet into his abominable flip-flops, the heretofore hearty but now worn to a ravelling traveller shakes his head and sighs.

"I think I may have lost my wallet," he mumbles.

The Customs Official cups a hand behind one ear, "Beg pardon?"

"Mister Customs Official, Sir," says the heretofore hearty but now worn to a ravelling traveller in a weary voice. "Unfortunately, I seem to have lost my wallet."

"Ah! Your passport, please." The Customs Official holds out a grasping hand, the heretofore hearty but now worn to a ravelling traveller roots through all his junk strewn on the table, picks out his passport, hands it to the Customs Official.

The Customs Official pulls out his stamp from a pocket, it comes down with an officious thwack and he hands the passport back smartly.

"You know," he says. "It would have saved us all a lot of time and trouble if you had confessed in the first place to having lost your wallet." Before the heretofore hearty but now worn to a ravelling traveller can reply, he makes his way back to the door and adds, "You are free to repack your luggage and leave by the side door. See that you do not linger around the airport."

With that, the Customs Official exits the small windowless room giving first the wallet not-so-secretly-secreted in his inside pocket a squeeze then his arse pocket another smart smack.

Meanwhile the heretofore hearty but now worn to a ravelling traveller scoops up his sombrero, pulls it down firmly on his head then repacks his bags as fast as he can, hoping that the ink has dried on all those sample foreign banknotes he had had printed so recently in the backstreets of Tangier.

Epilogue

So then, did 'they' finally catch up with the Customs Official...
Officer in the Service of Her Majesty the Queen? Was he brought
up before the Old Bill on charges of corruption and lining his own
pockets? Did the two neatly mustachioed gentlemen (the one
bearing a business-like smile, the other being in possession of rather
swarthy features) get their collars felt? And the hearty traveller?
Was he really the buffoon of a holiday-maker he made himself out
to be? Or, rather, was he a smuggler of dodgy foreign notes? And
finally... and maybe most importantly... who were the rather
dubious-looking ladies featured in the crumpled, well-thumbed
photographs?

www.ingramcontent.com/pod-product-compliance
Lightning Source LLC
Chambersburg PA
CBHW070349130626
46556CB00007B/3090